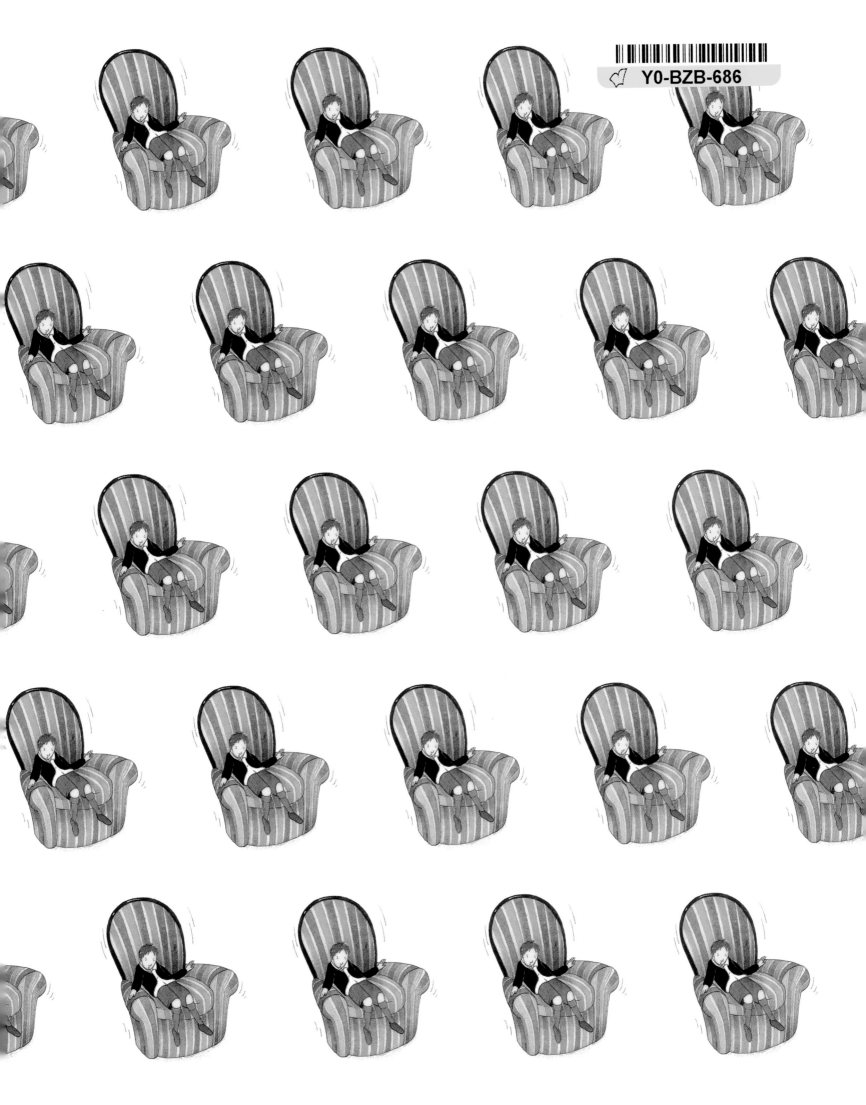

The Boy and the Spell

Library of Congress Cataloging-in-Publication Data

Shea, Pegi Deitz.
    The boy and the spell / adapted by Pegi Deitz Shea ; illustrated by Serena Riglietti. — 1st English ed.
        p. cm. — (Musical stories series ; #2)
"Based on the opera L'enfant et les sortilèges by Maurice Ravel, libretto by Colette."
    Summary: Sent to his bedroom for being naughty, a young boy throws a tantrum, injuring various objects in the room that later come to life to teach him a lesson. Based on the story from an opera by Maurice Ravel.
ISBN-13: 978-0-9646010-4-8
    [1. Behavior—Fiction. 2. Conduct of life—Fiction.]   I. Riglietti, Serena, ill. II. Ravel, Maurice, 1875-1937. Enfant et les sortilèges.
III. Colette, 1873-1954. Enfant et les sortilèges. IV. Title.
PZ7.S53755Bo 2007
[E]—dc22

                                     2006020249

10 9 8 7 6 5 4 3 2 1

Published by Pumpkin House, Ltd
P.O. Box 21373
Columbus, Ohio 43221

Design: Peri Poloni-Gabriel,
www.knockoutbooks.com

Printed in Singapore

The Boy and the Spell

Based on the opera by
Maurice Ravel, *libretto by* Colette

adapted by Pegi Deitz Shea   *illustrated by* Serena Riglietti

Pumpkin House

Thomas sat caged for hours. His math problems made him feel like a blockhead. Clock ticked him off, calling "cuckoo" five times. Melody Cat flicked him with her tail. Now Largo, the squirrel he had captured, was chattering "nutcase, nutcase, nutcase."

A knock—in the nick of time. His mother put down Thomas's snack and picked up his book. "Let's see your sums, Thomas. Oh my, haven't you solved anything, yet?"

"I, um, haven't had time."

"No time? Well, here is more time. Stay in your room until supper or until you've finished your work." And she closed the door behind her.

Thomas seethed. Time, I hate time. I wish there wasn't such a thing called time.

"Tock, tock," chuckled Clock.

Thomas couldn't take it anymore. Like a snare drum, his heart beat faster and faster—he couldn't help it!

CRASH!

Thomas sent Clock clattering to the floor. He tore up his books. Characters spilled out and scattered. Flaps lifted away! Words and numbers fled!

Thomas shredded the shepherd wallpaper, leaving the sheep in tatters. He shattered his plate and cup, the tea and milk splattering across the rug. Then *zingggg*, his dart found Largo's nose!

"Ouch!" the squirrel yipped.

"Too bad!" Thomas spat. He slumped into the lumpy chair and sighed at the sight of his room. "It's not my fault."

Suddenly, Armchair shook and groaned. "*Humph!* Think I will comfort you anytime you want, boy?"

"Who said that?" asked Thomas.

"Think you can kick my legs, punch my pillows and flatten my cushion with no repercussions?"

"Armchair?"

"Yes, it's me, young ruffian. And my stuffing has had enough!" Then Armchair took a huge breath and blew Thomas clear out of this world.

"Aaaah!" Thomas screamed, stumbling into a strange place in time.

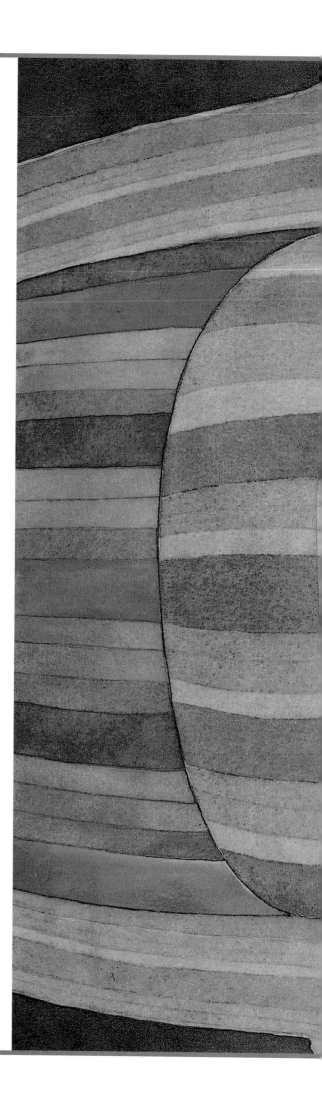

He landed, *plop,* face to face with Clock.

"What—*ding*—have you done?" Clock cried. "I'm all—*ding-ding*—out of time!"

"Stop chiming!" Thomas ordered. "Tell me, how many hours until supper?"

"I can't—*ding.* The hours have flown by. But look—*ding-ding-ding*—it must be tea time."

"Tea?" steamed Kettle. "Why should *we* bother? We bring him treats, then he flings us to the floor."

Thomas rubbed his scalded hand. "But I was mad!"

"You were bad!" Cake countered. "I say, let's dig into *him* for a change!"

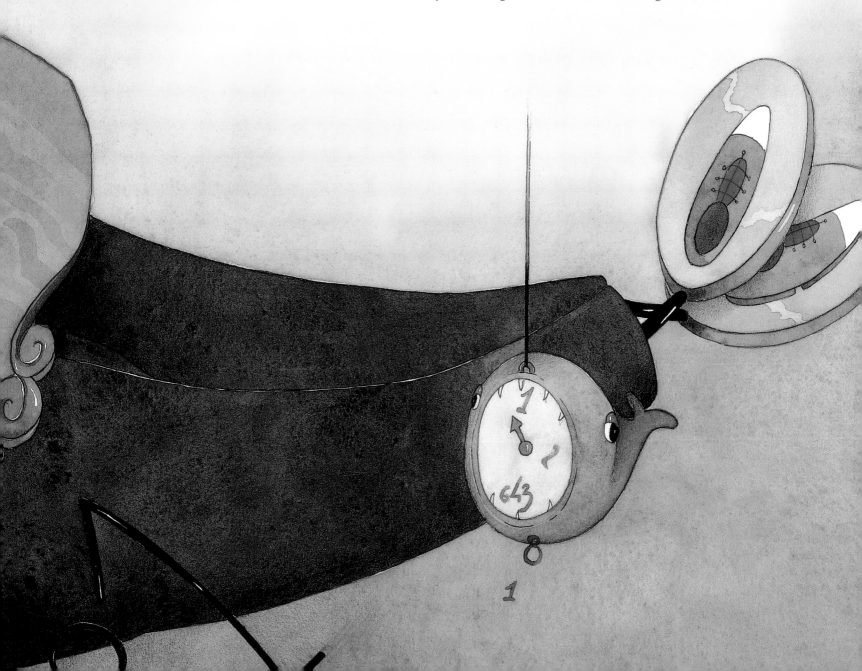

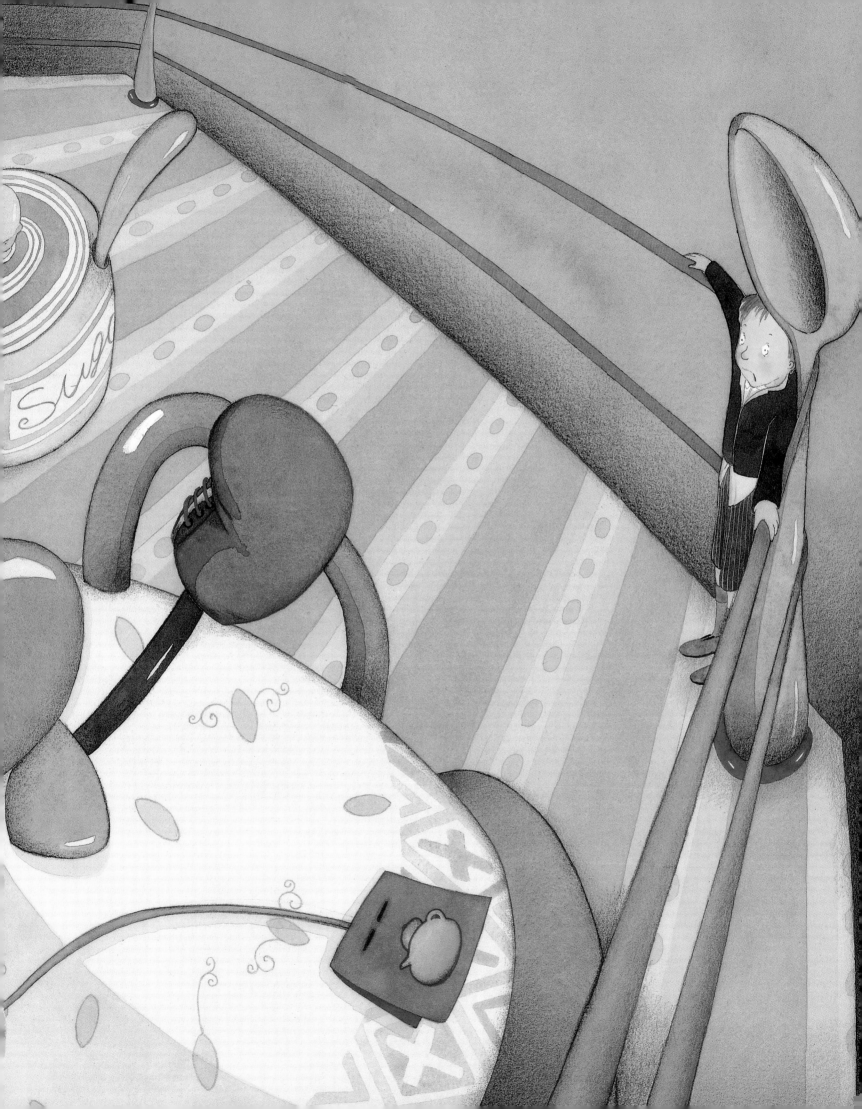

"Help, help!" Thomas called out to the shepherds who had been on the wallpaper. They were always nice and helpful. They even lent him sheep to count when he couldn't sleep.

But the shepherds didn't seem to hear Thomas. *They* were counting sheep this time, getting ready to leave.

Chair asked, "Where are you going?"

"To greener pastures," said the shepherd girl. "The boy has ripped us apart."

"He's torn my fabric, too," said Chair. "He used to be a nice boy."

"That's true. Remember his first smile?" asked the shepherd girl.

"I remember his first steps," said the shepherd boy.

"His first words," whistled Kettle.

"His first teeth," Cake said icily.

"Good-bye, good-bye," sang the shepherds, feeling blue. They strayed away, Thomas thought, like characters without their story.

"Story?" Thomas tore free of his reverie, and dove toward his favorite picture book. "Princess," he cried. "I need your help."

He opened the *Castle of Zabuda*. A broken tower popped, then flopped, and out shot a tiny princess into the clouds.

"Come back, Your Highness," Thomas called. "You can't leave the story."

"Methinks," she quivered, "that the Evil Enchanter is upon us."

"But how will the story end?" Thomas asked.

The princess shrugged. "If you mend Book's pages, I may return to find out."

When Thomas crumpled to the ground to rest, his math book fluttered open. Numerals tumbled out, bumbling into one another and tooting strange times-tables.

"Two times six is nine."

"Eleven times four is twenty."

"Three times twelve times three times five times one is one."

"That's not right," Thomas said, scratching his head.

"We know," said the numerals, riddled with confusion.

"Riddle?" Square Root asked. "If the train leaves Hartford on May Day, how many turkeys will have snowballs when the plane reaches the Bahamas? And don't forget to show your work."

"Ohhhh, my poor head," Thomas moaned, drifting off for forty winks.

He floated through a haunted forest. Lost pages tossed in the breeze. Trees waved good riddance. Thomas flew, suspended by the strings of a lute, borne on the breath of animal song. But the lyrics were full of sharp notes.

The animals had searched out Sage Owl. Below him, Thomas heard their complaints:

> He's flung five hundred fits,
> He's torn a million pages.
> He's hacked nine hundred branches.
> We're finished with his rages!

"Say no more, my woodland friends," Owl consoled them. "I have all the evidence I need to judge the boy. He has also yanked Melody's tail and pinned Dragonfly. And now Largo has gotten stuck trying to free herself. Friends, what are we going to do with this boy?"

Melody hissed, "I'll shear all his shorts."
Toady croaked, "I'll give him some warts."
Bat avowed, "I'll sneak a wee nip."
Fly suggested, "A big fat lip."

"Wait!" Thomas fell right into the midst of the animals.
He jumped to his feet and rushed to help Largo.

"Are you okay?" he asked, pulling Largo out of her cage. He held her tightly next to his heart.

"I didn't mean to hurt you. Or any of you," said Thomas, giving each a gentle pat. "I'm sorry."

When Thomas set Largo free, he heard the animals say, "That's a good boy."

"You know," said Owl, "if you want, you can see us every day in the forest."

"I'd like that," Thomas said.

Happily, the animals made plans to play the next day. Then they walked Thomas home.

All of a sudden, Thomas heard Clock chime five.

"Thomas!" his mother called upstairs.

"Mom!" he sang out.

He turned to say good-bye to his new friends, but they were already fading into the forest. That was okay. Thomas figured out himself how the story would end.

He sipped his tea, solved his problems before Clock struck six, and arrived at the supper table just in time.